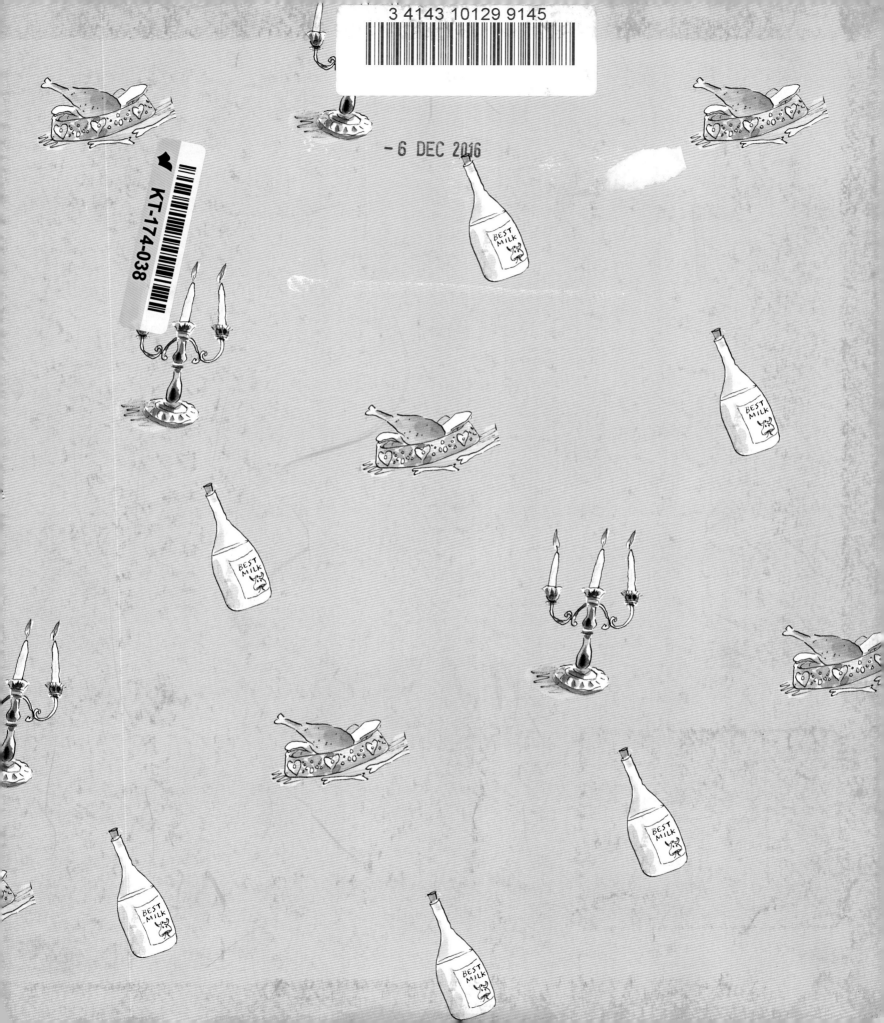

To Saffy, Stoker, Dexter, and Marilyn
and to the memories of Stanley, Sadie and Pippin.

First published in Great Britain in 2013 by Andersen Press Ltd.,

20 Vauxhall Bridge Road, London SW1V 2SA.

Published in Australia by Random House Australia Pty.,

Level 3, 100 Pacific Highway, North Sydney, NSW 2060.

Text and illustrations copyright © Tony Ross, 2013.

The rights of Tony Ross to be identified as the author and illustrator of this work

have been asserted by him in accordance with the Copyright, Designs and Patents Act, 1988.

All rights reserved. Colour separated in Switzerland by Photolitho AG, Zürich.

Printed and bound in Malaysia by Tien Wah Press.

Tony Ross has used pen, ink and watercolours in this book.

10   9   8   7   6   5   4   3   2   1

British Library Cataloguing in Publication Data available.

ISBN 978 1 84939 629 5

MIX
Paper from
responsible sources
FSC® C012700
FSC
www.fsc.org

This book has been printed on acid-free paper

Drat that Cat!

TONY ROSS

ANDERSEN PRESS

Suzy Cat lived with the Baggots,
so her full name was
Suzy Cat Baggot.

Mostly Suzy was well behaved . . .

. . . but sometimes, when she felt like it,
she could be really naughty.

Granddad didn't like cats, but cats liked him.
Suzy loved hopping onto his lap
and making his trousers all hairy.
"Drat that cat!" he would say.

Once she did a piddle in Dad's golf bag
and the smell wouldn't go away.
"Drat that cat!" he muttered.

When she bit Granddad on the ankle,
he fell over and landed on a squishy fur ball
that she had just sicked up.
"Drat that cat!" he bellowed.

When Mum bought a new sofa, Suzy thought
it was the best place to sharpen her claws.
Mum threw her out of the window, but she
came right back in and did it again!
"Drat that cat!"

Sometimes, the twins found warm cat poo
that Suzy had just buried in the garden.
"Eeeeuuuuuuuuuckk!" they squealed. "Drat that cat!"

Whenever anything bad happened,
Suzy got the blame . . .
. . . usually because she had done it.

Then one terrible day Suzy went off her food.
The twins put sticky, smelly Catslop on the ends
of their fingers and tried to get her to eat,
but Suzy just turned her head away.

Things got worse, when Suzy refused to drink.
Mum tried hard to dip her nose into her water bowl,
but she wriggled free.

Suzy just lay on the bed. She wouldn't open her eyes, she wouldn't eat and she wouldn't drink. Dad put her into the cat basket and took her to see the vet.

"What's the matter with you, then?" asked the vet.
Suzy didn't answer, she just looked sad.
"Better leave her with me," said the vet.

When Dad got home with the empty cat basket,
the twins began to cry. They even looked in the garden
for a nice place to bury Suzy beside Snail and Frog.
"She's not dead yet!" said Dad.

The house seemed very empty without Suzy. Nobody spoke
at supper. It would have been nice to warm up a mouse for her.

Two days later, the vet phoned, to say that Suzy was better!
Granddad took the twins to collect her.

Everybody made a fuss of her when she got home.
The twins took her into the garden to play digging games.
Dad let her sleep in his golf bag, and Mum was even happy
to see her sharpening her claws on the new sofa.

Suzy was allowed to eat at the table.
Instead of Catslop, she was given the very best chicken,
served in the new dish that Granddad had bought specially.

After supper, Suzy went for her evening
stroll in the garden. Mum opened the door for her.
"Don't do anything I wouldn't do!" called Granddad.
"Come back soon," said Dad.

Suzy went next door to see Charlie Dog.
"Are you OK now?" he woofed.
"I'm fine," said Suzy.
"Why do you ask?"

"Well, we all heard
you were dreadfully ill
and wouldn't eat or drink,"
said Charlie Dog.

"Oh, I was just *pretending*," said Suzy.
"Really, I hopped over here and ate your
Dogslop and water. Sorry!"
"Hmm, I wondered where they went,"
said Charlie Dog. "But why did you do that?"

"Ah," purred Suzy with a secret smile. "I wanted them to know JUST how much they love me!"

Drat that cat!